Dedicated to my son.

"May this book encourage you to have love for reading the Quran."

Love,
Mommy

I invited ب, ت, and ث to play on the umbrella at Masjid An-Nabawi in Madinah.

Come play! Come play!
Soon to join are siblings
ج, ح and خ.

Here to stay are cool kids
د and ذ up the umbrella of
our beloved masjid!

Come play! Come play!
Brother ر climbs up
with big bro ز. See ya!

س and ش can be seen
running to the umbrella at
Masjid An-Nabawi.
Come play! Come play!

Here come friends ص, ض, ط, and ظ to play together at the masjid of our dear prophet Muhammad (PBUH).

Come play! Come play! ع asks غ to race him to the top of the umbrella!

"Don't forget us!" call ف, ق and ك as they climb back to back.

All the little letters are jumping and playing on the flaps of the umbrella in Madinah!

Hopping their way are ل and م. Where had they been?

Boom! Now comes ن!
"Wow! Wait for me!"
says و. Soon laughing
"hahaha," slides in ه!

ﺱ

Come play! Come play!
"Here I come!" calls ﺀ.
"Yeah, what about me?"
asks ﻯ ---

All the little letters slide to the ground as the umbrella closes its flaps at sundown.